ISBN: 9798858150763

REAL
SHORT

STORIES
FOR SENIORS

VOLUME III

Haleigh Brown

CHAMELEON
PUBLICATIONS

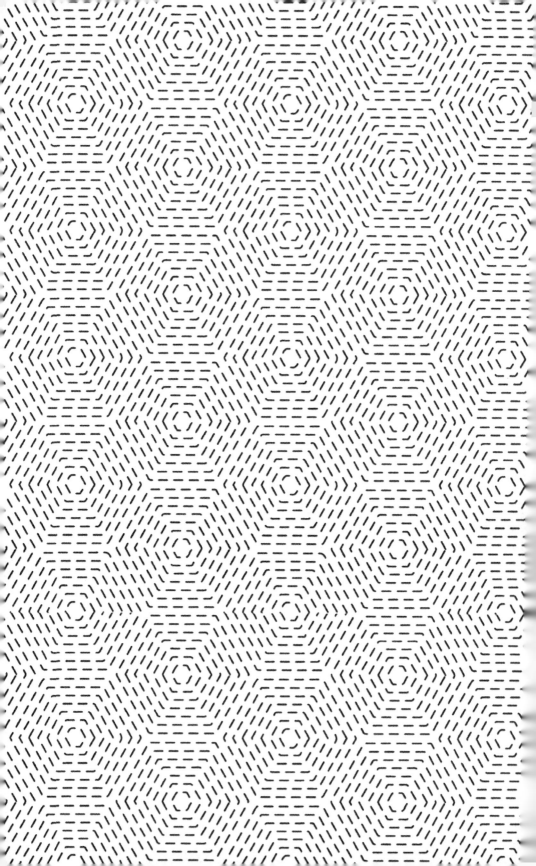

CONTENTS

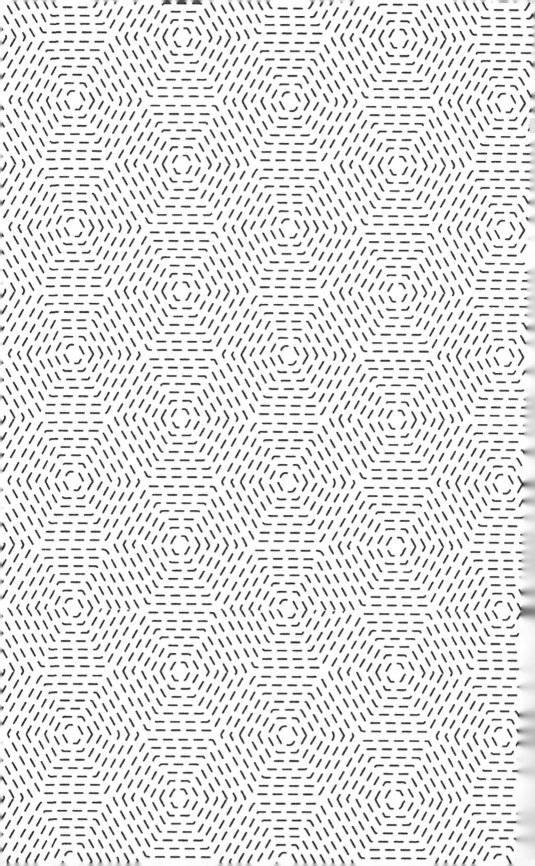

SISTERS ON THE COURT

"Do you think we can win?" Serena asked her older sister, Venus. Tennis was their passion. They both had awards to prove their skill should not be underestimated. Still, Serena was nervous. This would be the first time they were playing a game of doubles together. It wasn't any regular match, either. The sisters were playing for an Olympic gold medal.

Venus smirked and set down her racket. "You and I both know we can win."

It was no secret that Venus held the power on the court when it came to playing other pairs. It quickly became what she was known for. Serena knew that should ease her mind, but somehow it added to the pressure of the tennis match.

The two sisters walked out to the court with their heads held high. Venus looked as confident as ever as she led the way. Being fifteen months older, she joked that she was more dominant than Serena. Most people were more surprised to hear that they weren't twins, considering many assumed so.

"We've got this," Venus said to her younger sister as they split apart. A big smile filled her face. Serena smiled back.

It was much easier to accept a potential loss when it was her playing on the court. The only one who was let down in that situation was herself. But adding Venus into the mix still worried her. If they lost the match, would her sister ever want to play doubles with her again? How would her older sister react if they didn't win the gold medal because of her?

Without any more time to worry, Serena needed to focus. She reminded herself of her success. She held 23 Grand Slam titles for single matches.

"I can do this," she whispered under her breath. Then she looked at her older sister staring at their opponents. "We can do this," she repeated what Venus said.

As soon as the first ball came towards her, Serena zoned in on the game. Nothing could break her focus. She realized she played just as well with her sister by her side. Both sisters had an unspoken bond on the court. During practice, they both felt it. But it was even more noticeable in the heat of their competition.

Serena noticed that the other pair was growing tired quickly. Each hit of the ball from her and Venus sent the other players scrambling to hit the ball. When the other players missed two balls in a row, Venus looked back at her. They were on the path to victory.

In their final set, Serena scored the last winning point. She didn't even hear the announcer call their win because Venus was tackling her with a hug.

"We did it!" she cheered.

Serena was thrilled to win the gold medal, especially alongside her sister. While it felt like a test of their relationship, she learned that their passion for tennis was just as strong together as it was separate.

PLAYING HOOKY FOR GOOD

Surrounded by snow, I sat on the steps of the Swedish Parliament. I held a sign that explained what I was doing in a few words: School Strike for Climate. It was the only way for adults to start taking me seriously while I voiced my concerns about climate change. It even took time for members of the legislature to notice me.

One man in particular stood in front of me, reading my sign with a sharp look of judgment.

"Playing hooky from school?" he asked.

"Yes," I answered back. But he was still perplexed that I was sitting outside of the parliament building rather than making the most of a day off from school.

Little did he know, it was not the first or last day I was on strike from school for the cause.

He started to walk away, and I stopped him. "I am on a school strike for the climate. Nobody listens. We need to act now."

I could tell he underestimated me. It was the same reaction from most adults.

"Explain," he demanded. "Why now?"

I jumped at the chance for someone to hear me out. Of course I had support from the adults closest to me like my parents and other relatives. But someone associated with the legislature could help the movement in a much more meaningful way, which was my entire goal with the strike.

"The effects of climate change are already happening. There are rising temperatures globally and unusual patterns of weather. These impact sea levels and how crops around the world grow. Not to mention the quality of life for humans," I explained. I hoped that I didn't lose his interest yet.

He looked intrigued as I spoke.

Before he could ask another question, I continued. "We need regulations and action to lower our role. The more places in the world that take action, the better outcome we will have."

"Why does this mean so much to you? You're just a kid." The man began to smile, and I feared my explanation did nothing to convince him of my goal. All because I was young… I was just a kid with a voice that wasn't loud enough.

"That is exactly why it means so much to me. I'm just a kid and there are generations that will continue to grow up in this world after you. Our future is on the line if we do not act." My voice grew stronger. I flipped his argument.

The reason he thought I should not care was the exact reason I did care.

I saw his attitude change directly in front of my eyes. That was when I felt true hope in the fight I cared so much about.

"I think more people need to hear you say that," he said.

That moment changed everything for me. I went on to speak in front of more members of the parliament and eventually collaborated with a British environmental group. Together, we pushed for a law to require the country to lower its carbon footprint.

Despite all of the doubt, and jokes about me playing hooky, actionable steps were taken on behalf of climate change. It all started with playing hooky but for a good cause.

BARBIE'S WORLD

Ruth watched her daughter scribble on the paper cut out. She'd spend the evening helping her daughter draw and cut out dolls from paper. She didn't quite understand it right away, but her daughter didn't want to play with baby dolls. She said she was tired of taking care of babies and wanted to play with dolls that were more fun. Ruth colored in a pink dress on one of the paper dolls. She realized there weren't a set of dolls that represented women in careers to young girls.

"What if there were dolls like this that weren't made from paper?" she asked her daughter.

"I'd like that," she replied.

That was all it took for the gears in Ruth's mind to turn. She was the co-founder of the toy giant Mattel, alongside her husband Elliot. This special role gave them both expert insight into the toy industry. Ruth had never considered that young girls wanted to play with dolls that were different than them. The only woman doll that she knew of was sold in tobacco stores as a gag gift. Nobody took it seriously. But Ruth believed the womanly doll could make all of the difference for young girls.

She told one friend, "We've seen young girls tend to baby dolls like they are mothers. We should show them women in different roles that could also shape their future."

Ruth's idea certainly was different than those of others who worked at Mattel. She couldn't be certain how the idea would strike them. But to her surprise, there was much more support than anticipated. Mattel got to work transforming the gag-gift doll into a toy for children. Her name was Barbara, and she would go by Barbie. The very first doll to debut at the American Toy Fair in New York City on March 9, 1959. Ruth saw her idea come to life. Barbie's very first role was mimicking the popular style of glamour in the 1950s, like Marilyn Monroe.

Ruth never could have imagined how much of success

Barbie would be in the first year, as over 300,000 dolls were sold. People were fascinated by the doll, both adults and children. Especially Ruth and Elliot's daughter who saw the very first prototype. Ruth would never forget the joy the doll brought her daughter. Mattel continued creating more and incorporating more of Ruth's ideas to present Barbie as a woman of many different roles.

Over the years, Barbie had more than 250 careers including pilot, engineer, rockstar, president, astronaut, and teacher. The doll proved to show girls from a young age that women could fill these roles. It gave them an image of what a woman would look like in these career paths. Without Barbie, young girls would have missed out on the firsthand view of what women can accomplish. Girls learned that Barbie's world could be their own one day.

THE REBEL OF FASHION

Coco stared at her row of mannequins, all dressed in her clothing designs. They weren't the typical designs for women's clothing in the mid-1920s. She was proud of her designs; even though she spent time explaining her reasoning for her designs to her critics. Coco's approach to women's fashion came from what she enjoyed wearing, and her priority of comfort.

Another designer at the time enjoyed pointing out the differences, even taunting Coco that any fashion trend that favored her clothing would eventually fade.

"Everything is baggy, like men's clothing," the designer once told Coco. "Why bother making these at all? Just hand women their husband's clothing."

"They can have their own clothing that is like this," Coco said. She firmly believed that she wasn't the only woman in the world who enjoyed loose pants. Before designing her own pair of baggy women's pants, Coco had a habit of stealing her lovers' pants as a keepsake.

The design of her loose-fitting pants became known as beach pajamas. She was first seen wearing them while on a tropical vacation. They were flowy and comfortable. Coco was inspired by the shape and cut of Sailor's pants at the time and used them as inspiration for her design.

"They look like pajamas," another designer told her. They seemed to be shocked that she had designed clothing that looked to be associated with the bedroom.

But all of the chatter and comments that Coco received didn't change her approach. She was a seamstress long before she had the pleasure of designing her own clothing. This was a passion for Coco. She was certain she had value in the fashion world and wasn't going to let anyone talk her out of it, simply because her designs were different.

In an interview, Coco explained her logic. "Women's clothing doesn't need to be all silk and satin or formfitting. There isn't anything more beautiful than a body with freedom."

While the outside world had opinions about her, Coco stayed true. She continued to create clothing that was comfortable and trendy for women in brand new ways. It was her goal to see women in clothing that worked with all areas of their lives, whether they were career women or homemakers.

Coco Chanel eventually became a household name. Aside from the pants, she went on to create new styles for women, many of which were inspired by men's clothing. Such as the nautical top. Coco enjoyed the look of the striped sweaters worn by sailors and fishermen and created a new style for women that clashed with the earlier designs. Coco also created the first two-piece suit for women and a special scent of perfume. She believed the scent smelled like a woman, and not like all of the others on the market that smelled like flowers.

Without Coco's new way of thinking, we may have never seen such fashion trends that still are alive today. Women's comfort in their clothing likely would have remained a controversial topic. The stiff clothing that was uncomfortable likely would have stayed the norm for many decades to pass. But Coco never let the doubt of others change her designs.

FROM THE FARM TO SPACE

Yuri Gagarin never could have imagined he would be the first person in space. His life was simple from a very young age. As the son of a carpenter, his father always instilled in him the value of hard work.

"No cutting corners," he would tell Yuri. For a long time, Yuri felt his father was always too hard on him. He thought his father was a man who paid far too much attention to the little details.

As a young boy and teenager, Yuri spent nearly all his time working on the farm. The winters were freezing, and the summers felt like they would never end. But he pressed forward and kept his father's words in mind. Yuri was a survivor of the Nazi occupation of Russia and went on to join the Soviet Air Force in 1955.

His dream was to become a pilot and thanks to all of the lessons he learned from his father and working on the farm, he knew what he needed to do to achieve that goal. He worked hard and stayed focused on the small details that others missed while in the Air Force. It made him both a better man and a better pilot.

In only a few years, Yuri received a new title.

His chief presented him with the news. "You're one of the top pilots in the country," he told him. Yuri was in awe. He loved flying and believed it was what he was supposed to do with his life. But little did he know he would soon receive news of something even bigger from his chief—a flight that would change everything. The news was that Yuri was selected to go to space on the spacecraft Vostok 1 in a very dangerous mission.

Yuri never considered himself an astronaut, but his pilot skills were exactly what was needed to make a trip to space. On April 12, 1961, Yuri was lifted into space and deemed the first human to leave Earth and orbit in space. He was nervous about the flight, but more excited than anything. To him, this was a test of his piloting skill. His name would be a permanent part of history.

"It will change history for the entire world. Not just me," he told a pilot close to him before lifting off.

His orbit lasted 1 hour and 48 minutes and he lost radio contact with Earth for 23 minutes. In those silent moments, he stayed true to his confidence.

"I'm one of the top pilots in my country," he said to himself. Space was new territory for him, but he leaned into his skills. In the big picture, this flight wasn't much different from the hundreds he'd completed before.

Yuri landed successfully in the Soviet Union by parachute and quickly became one of the biggest celebrities in the Soviet Union. It all felt like a dream to Yuri. During his orbit, he thought of himself in the past. He was a young boy working hard on the farm. Back then he worried he may not survive the Nazis. However, his skill and work ethic got him one of the most incredible titles in the world: the very first human in space.

SOMETHING MUST CHANGE

When Candy Lightner lost her thirteen-year-old daughter, Cari, unexpectedly, she thought she would never be the same.

"If she is gone, what else do I have to live for?" she asked her best friend over tea. It was the first day she'd managed to socialize since her daughter passed away.

Her friend gently held her hand. "Cari would want you to live your life to the fullest."

Candy knew her friend was right. But she was still stumped on what to do about it. How could she live her life to the fullest? The accident that took Cari's life was preventable. It never should have happened. A man driving while under the influence of alcohol took her daughter's life.

Candy tried to explain that to her friend. "I'm not alone in this," she said. Then explained some information she read. In the same year, there were approximately 27,000 alcohol-related traffic fatalities occurred in the United States, including 2,500 in California.

Her friend was shocked. "I had no idea it was so common."

"Drunk driving is not prosecuted harshly," Candy said. "But something must change."

Candy used the loss of her daughter to propel her forward. She wanted to create a massive change in the American justice system.

"You have the power to make change…" Candy's best friend knew her better than anyone. She was right.

Candy wanted to start by gathering people who experienced what she did so closely. She established the group Mothers Against Drunk Driving (MADD) where a small group of women impacted could meet. It was finally a safe space for all of them to connect. There was no need to explain the pain and frustration of their loss. They understood each other right away.

With the group formed, Candy informed them of her next plan. "The only way real progress will happen is if the laws change."

The other mothers agreed with her. The issue of drunk driving needed to be met with stronger punishments. Candy began lobbying the Governor of California.

"Our state needs a task force," she said. "One that will investigate these cases of drunk driving."

The governor eventually agreed with her and picked her to be the very first member of this task force. Not long after, President Ronald Reagan asked Candy to serve on the National Commission on Drunk Driving. In July of 1984, Candy stood next to the president as he signed a law to drive states to raise the drinking age to 21.

"This change is estimated to save about 800 traffic deaths annually," Candy stated, on behalf of the commission group. Within one year, all 50 states had reformed their drunk-driving laws.

It only took a few years for Candy to see the impact of her nonprofit group in action. The changes she proposed were no longer only in her home state of California but across the entire country. She did something to save the lives of others and prevent the tragedy she knew all too well.

At a time when Candy wasn't sure what to do, she demanded changes for the better.

WHERE DREAMS ARE MADE

As a young boy, I always heard stories about a place far away from Hungary. It was magical. My grandparents said they would never be able to see it, but that maybe I could in my lifetime. I asked them a lot of questions about this place. What did it look like? How far away was it? What would I have to do to visit?

My grandfather would smile and say, "Thomas, you will have to see that for yourself. Only a man who has seen it with his own two eyes will know."

His empty reply frustrated me. I wanted him to tell me all of the details. But as I grew older, I began to understand my grandfather's perspective. I no longer wanted him to tell me about the place, known as America. Instead, I needed to see it for myself. Going to America felt like a dream in itself. I couldn't imagine accomplishing more dreams of mine simply by being there.

In the 1960s, long after my grandparents passed away, society continued to shift. Communism was strong and I wanted to escape Hungary. Part of me was fearful to leave behind everything I knew. It was my home and the history of my family ran deep. Still, I wanted more for my life. I wanted to see America with my own eyes as a grown man.

I made the promise to myself and even prayed to my grandparents about taking the risk. The path to America was not a clean-cut one, but I would manage. All I had on my back was a small bag with food and a photo of my grandparents.

I stared at the photo. Tears burned behind my eyelids. "This will keep me going."

I left Hungary behind in the dark of night. I walked for miles and managed to get on one of the ships sailing to America. The days blended together. I was unsure how long it had been.

I kept to myself and skipped meals. I did anything to blend in with the other workers on the ship. Some spoke English, which I didn't have much skill in yet.

When the ship docked on the northeastern coast of North America, I thought of my grandfather. I finally knew what he meant. I did what no man in our family had done—I saw America with my own two eyes, and it was incredible. That was when my life truly began.

I jumped into working any job I could find and began teaching myself English. If someone took a chance on me for work, I gladly accepted. Then, while landscaping an area near Central Park in New York City, I met the man that would change my life. He introduced me to computer programming.

"Computers speak their own language to work. If you can teach yourself English as well as you have, I have no doubt you can learn computer programming." The man had confidence in me already. Between my long hours and various jobs, I made time to study with him. I even built my first computer with his help.

I looked at the photograph of my grandparents. It survived the trip to America with me and became my most prized possession.

"Your grandson is becoming a computer program-mer...in America." Imagining their smiles and pride made me tear up again.

Several years later, I had enough savings from work-ing as a programmer and labor jobs to purchase a computer programming company. With a bit of extra work, the company quickly became profitable. The success of it changed my life. I went from a man immigrating to the United States with nothing to a man worth $12.6 billion.

FOOD FOR THOUGHT

It was my senior year in college at the University of Maryland. The campus had become my home over the years as I studied hard to receive a degree in Journalism. One day, I sat with a group of my peers in the dining hall. It was our routine to keep our notes or textbooks open even while we ate.

In the distance, I watched as the staff of the dining hall gathered the remaining food from their containers. The man scraped all of the food into trash bags.

"What are you looking at?" Evan asked me.

I didn't realize that I was staring at the food get thrown away. But it bothered me.

"Have you guys ever noticed how much food goes to waste at the end of the day?" I asked my peers. Cam and Mia paused, then nodded.

"Yes, I have seen that in the morning, too," Mia said.

"It's perfectly good food. It shouldn't get thrown away," I replied. My ideas began to run wild in my mind. What if we could find a solution to this?

Studying Journalism made me more confident in approaching people. So, without looking back, I approached the staff of the dining hall.

"Excuse me. Do you ever keep any of this food? To give away?" I asked the man.

He shook his head. That was when I realized we would need to approach someone higher up at the university who could answer my questions. And more importantly, help find a solution to food waste coming from my campus.

The following day, I went to the dean of the school to pitch my idea of donating the leftover food. Mia, Cam, and Evan joined me. We all agreed something needed to be done about the amount of food waste. There were hungry people both on and off campus who could eat the food that was already prepared. I hoped that my university would see the benefit of donating the food.

Our meeting didn't last long. "I will look into the issue and see if solutions can be made," the dean didn't seem as excited as we were to create a change. But it was better than nothing.

Cam, Evan, Mia, and I began collecting more data on the issue of hunger. We even prepared signs to protest the issue if we needed to. Many other students heard about our idea and thought it was a waste of time.

"The dining hall food isn't even that good," one girl said. "You can't even give that food away."

She wasn't the only one to say such comments about our efforts. But it fueled the four of us to prove them wrong. It only took a few weeks for the university to approve our plans to create what we called Food Recovery Network. The dining hall immediately put a plan together to store the leftover food each day and work with us to distribute it to those in need.

By the end of the school year, Food Recovery Network had recovered 30,000 meals to all different nonprofit organizations centered around ending hunger. The meals cooked in our dining hall fed citizens across the DC area. Any other students or administrators who doubted the idea were proven wrong when Food Recovery Network branched out to create chapters across America. It even was named the largest student movement against hunger and food waste in the country, thanks to the students who knew the food could be enough to save the lives of others.

LOVE YOUR NEIGHBOR

I pushed the stroller in the grocery store. There wouldn't be much that I could afford, but I needed to find something for my kids. We were new to this side of town, and the little bit of money I had was used up in the move. Walking up and down the aisles of food, I scanned the prices.

My son grabbed a box of cereal, one with a prize inside the box. "Please, Dad! Please!"

A woman moved by me, giving me a polite smile as she reached for something from the top shelf. It pained me to tell my son no, especially for food and in front of a stranger.

I grabbed the box of cereal that was on sale. "We need to get this one, Brandon."

He started to cry, and my younger son joined in. "Why?"

My cheeks burned red. "It's on sale." Honestly, buying cereal at all was a splurge. The small amount of cash I had to spend on food needed to go to the essentials.

The woman that passed by reached over to grab the cereal that my son put back. "I'll get this for your boys." She gave me a kind smile.

"You don't need to do that—" I said, but she was already placing it in her basket. "Do you need anything else? How about some milk?"

A wave of relief washed over me. I said yes before I could argue with myself.

The woman introduced herself as Julia Wise. I told her we just moved to the neighborhood and I was struggling with money. Julia filled her shopping cart with more items for us, even when I assured her she didn't have to.

"My husband Jeff and I do things like this a lot. We really like to help." She grinned.

At the checkout, Julia paid for everything. She refused to accept the cash I offered to cover part of the cost.

"Keep your money," she told me.

Tears filled my eyes as I grabbed the full shopping bags. We had food to fill the cabinets of our new home. I didn't have to scramble to feed my sons or go to bed hungry myself. Outside the store, I thanked Julia and asked her about her husband.

"Jeff and I set aside money from our income to do this," she said after I questioned her. "We donate a lot to causes in other countries. But helping our neighbors is equally as important."

My youngest son looked up at her and smiled from the stroller.

Once back home, I searched for her and Jeff's names on the internet. A local tribune article came up, where our small town wrote a piece about their charity efforts. Julia Wise and Jeff Kaufman donated 40% of their income to those less fortunate every year.

I was shocked to know that I crossed paths with someone so generous. Julia and Jeff's kindness helped people across the world and in their very own small town.

THE DONOR

I couldn't believe it when my doctor called me with the news. "Brenda, we've received a liver that is a match for you."

Tears of joy spilled down my cheeks. It took almost a year of waiting to finally be matched with a new liver. Mine was failing and my health was declining. I knew I needed a match sooner than later. But then, I was shocked when my doctor called me again.

"Brenda, I don't normally do this. But I wanted to ask you something."

His words worried me. "What is it?"

"A young woman is also at the hospital in need of

a liver. At this rate, she only has a day to live without one. I'm not sure if this will change your mind about the match," he explained.

I had a decision to make. "How old is she?"

"Twenty-three," he replied.

She was so young compared to me, at 68 years old. She had an entire life ahead of her until this emergency struck. I was nervous another match might not come in time for me if I passed up the liver. But I couldn't imagine the young woman dying at such a young age.

"Give her the kidney," I said.

"Are you sure?" he asked. "You will remain on the list to receive one. But it could take a long time again."

"I understand that. Give it to her. Save her life."

Part of me couldn't believe what I said. I was passing up the liver that I had been praying for. What if mine completely failed before I got another match? Would I regret this decision?

I let myself worry for a little while, but my decision held strong. I could wait a little longer if it meant saving someone else's life today. How selfish it would be if I took it for myself! All I could hope was that the young woman made a full recovery and went on to live the rest of her life.

Four days later, I received another call from my doctor. "Brenda, we've received another liver match for you."

My jaw fell open. "Already?" I asked. I had been preparing myself for another 6 months or even a year of waiting again. "It's only been four days."

I could hear my doctor's smile through the phone. "It's quite the miracle, isn't it?"

Before my surgery, the young woman asked if she could meet me. Her name was Abigail and she looked even younger than twenty-three.

"Thank you," she beamed at me. "Without you, I wouldn't be here."

I shook my head. "Don't thank me. We can thank the donor who was a match to begin with. Plus, the new donor with my liver."

We both began to cry with gratitude.

"You have the rest of your life ahead of you. Live every day like it counts, because it does." I probably didn't need to tell her that, considering she came so close to dying. But I also decided to take my own advice. Just because I was 68 didn't mean I couldn't live the rest of my life to the fullest too.

Giving up the first liver to Abigail was the best thing I could have done.

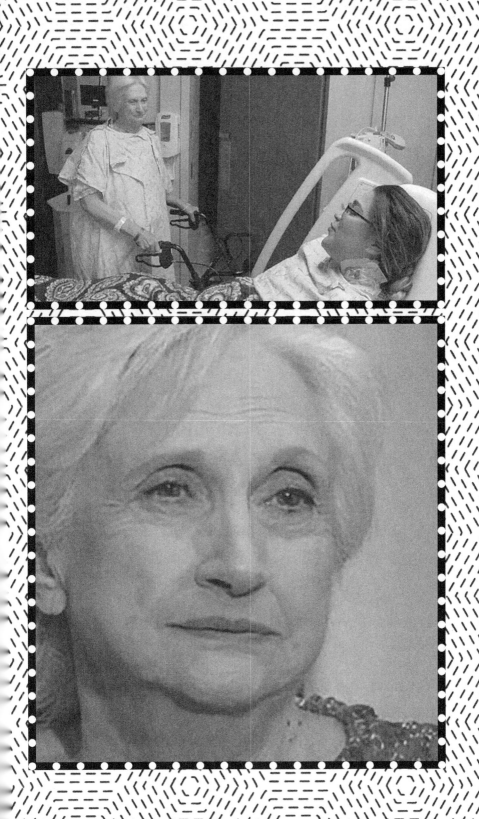

HERO TURNED FRIEND

Molly wasn't sure what to do. She looked at her fifteen-year-old daughter and only felt worried. She received the diagnosis of a severe form of kidney disease, which could take her life if she didn't receive a donor's kidney. That would leave her young teenage daughter without a mother.

"I can't let that happen," she said to herself one morning. She wanted to stay alive for herself, but even more so for her daughter.

With her doctor's help, she sought out potential kidney donors. But when she failed to find a match, she needed to take the search into her own hands. In her last attempt, she turned to social media. She wrote out her story, her search for a kidney donor, and shared it with the world through the Internet.

Molly didn't want to tell the entire world about her battle. However, it felt like the only option to find a match. Maybe someone in her city or state could be a donor match. She wanted to do whatever it took to stay alive for her daughter.

After making the public post, Molly lay in bed. She was sad that she was so desperate, but then she thought about her daughter's smiling face. A new kidney meant she could see that smile over and over again. She would live to see her daughter graduate high school, go to college, and maybe even get married one day.

In the silence of her bedroom, she promised herself, "It will all be worth it."

Molly asked any potential donors to email her. But she waited three days before checking her account. What if there weren't any emails? What if her plea went unanswered?

Once she read her emails, Molly couldn't have been more wrong. She had a very special person who offered to donate a kidney to her. It was her friend, Krisi. But Kristi was no ordinary friend. Molly met her when she was the paramedic who saved Molly's dad's life seven years prior when he was in cardiac arrest. Molly and

Kristi became friends when she wanted to express her gratitude for saving her father's life.

Molly met up with Kristi to talk to her about her offer.

"Are you sure about this?" Molly asked her friend. Donating a kidney was no small venture.

Kristi beamed. "Of course I am sure. You deserve to live… to see your daughter grow and meet your grandkids."

Molly was shocked to know that the woman who saved her father's life was about to save hers, too.

Shortly after their meeting, Kristi discovered she was a perfect match for Molly. The surgery could be done and turned out to be a complete success. Molly was beyond grateful for Kristi's kindness and sacrifice. She was a hero, who turned into a dear friend. Molly never could have known seven years prior when she saved her father's life that Kristi would save her own life one day, too.

All Kristi could say about Molly and her family was, "They have a piece of my heart."

SURVIVING THE WILDERNESS

Three days had passed since I last saw my family. I only knew that because the sky had gone dark three times and I had to find a place to hide for the night in the woods. I didn't know where I was or how I'd become lost in the wilderness of Queensland.

My partner and I went on a drive and stopped at a rest stop. They stopped to visit a friend, and I'd decided to go for a hike in the nearby land. There was a sign that indicated there was a swimming hole. In the blistering heat, a dip in the water sounded refreshing.

However, I made it to the water and when I turned to walk back, I realized I could not find the rest stop. I walked for what felt like hours. Instead of the trees and shrubs lessening, they only grew thicker.

A harsh realization hit me. "I am lost," I whispered as the chirps of crickets echoed around me.

I hoped that hiking through the wilderness would become easier. But it didn't. I cut my feet and arms, and the dizziness left me disoriented. At times, I wondered if I was walking in the same circles over and over. A small part of me wanted to lie beneath a set of trees and give up. Mother Nature was much stronger than me.

But I pictured my four kids' faces. I couldn't stand the thought of never seeing them again.

"I'm not giving up," I told myself, pushing through the weakness of my body. I looked around in the wilderness and decided to try a new route. There was a small clearing of trees and I hoped for the best as I walked through it.

A small wooden fence caught my eye. "Is that real?" I wondered, unsure if I could trust my vision. I ran towards the small ranch. The bottoms of my feet burned and ached with every step. But, if there was someone at that ranch, they could help me find my family.

I ran across the property, and couldn't find anybody to help me. But I did spot a small, off-road vehicle. Was I really about to steal it to find help for myself? Of course I was!

I drove through the brush and dirt and spotted a sign. When I slowed down, I could hear cars driving. I drove down a path and followed the sound. It led to the edge of one of the main freeways in Queensland. A rancher stopped to help me, and I learned there was a search party looking for me for eight days.

After receiving medical care, I was reunited with my partner and four children. The local detectives said it was quite a miracle I survived. They asked what kept me going through the heat, injuries, and confusion during those long days.

I replied to them with a smile, "The thought of seeing my children again. It helped me survive the wilderness."

A NEW LIFE ON THE LINE

Working as a 9-1-1 operator was always an intense job. Speaking with people during the time of an emergency was difficult. However, it was also very fulfilling. I was able to provide support for those and assure them that help would soon arrive. During the job, I spoke with people in many different situations. But one stood out to me in a way like no other.

I was going into the seventh hour of my shift, and quite tired. When I answered the particular call, I could immediately tell the man calling in was very distraught. I even struggled to understand him at first.

"Sir, take a deep breath," I told him calmly. "Explain to me what has happened."

He wasn't able to take a deep breath, and instead shouted, "My wife! She's in labor!"

Out of every call I took in my time working as an operator, I'd never spoken to anyone through labor. I asked him his location and dispatched the paramedics right away.

"The paramedics will be there shortly. Make sure your wife is taking deep breaths." I promised him. But I could hear his wife groaning in the background and wondered how much time there was left before the baby was born. That was the moment I realized I may need to walk him through the delivery process. There was a new life on the line.

"He needs to come out! My son!" he yelled and then instructed his wife to take deep breaths.

"Is she in a comfortable position? You may need to deliver him if he is that close to being born."

"How do I do that?!" The man's voice echoed through the phone. I could hear the fear as his voice trembled.

"You've got her comfortable and taking deep breaths. You can now tell her to push if you are prepared to get the baby if he comes out," I explained.

He was quiet for a moment. I could tell it was because he was uncertain.

"You can do this!" I promised him. "Help will be there any minute to assist you."

"Okay," he sighed. I waited patiently while he told his wife to push. Within moments, I heard the overwhelming sound of a newborn crying.

"I have him! My son!" The man cried out in joy. "He's here!"

"How does he look? And your wife?" I asked.

"Both happy and healthy!" The man replied, then said he was handing the newborn to his wife. Then I could hear him speaking to the paramedics in the background as he let them inside.

"They'll be in for a surprise. But don't worry, they'll check over your wife and son and ensure everyone is good."

"Thank you so much for your help. I couldn't have done it without you!"

I smiled as his comment. "Of course you could have," I told him. I wished him the best with his new family and disconnected the call. I was proud of myself for staying calm as I instructed him. But really, the new father had done all of the work himself.

Like every other call I'd taken before, I thought it would end there. Little did I know, the family of three would be standing in front of me a few weeks later.

My supervisor stopped me on my lunch break and said, "Katie, you have some surprise visitors who would like to meet you."

The family hadn't crossed my mind, but as soon as I saw the newborn baby I the arms of his father, I knew who it was.

"We just wanted to thank you for your help," his mother said to me.

"Of course! I am so happy everything was a success," I said and looked at the baby. "He is beautiful!"

THE WOMAN'S VOICE

Over the radio, I heard the report come in about an abandoned vehicle in the river. My long shift was almost over, and I thought about ending my shift there. I looked at my partner who was gearing up to drive to the scene.

"Are you coming or clocking out?" he asked.

I shrugged. "I'll come along for this last one."

The 2016 winter in Utah was particularly brutal. The snowstorms were coming back to back almost daily and most of the calls we got were weather-related. An abandoned car was no surprise. I felt myself growing more tired and almost regretful that I went out on another call.

"A fisherman called this in?" I asked my partner as we stepped out of the truck.

"Yep," he replied. "The water is completely frozen. Can't imagine the fish are too good." His joke made me smile.

We rushed through the snow towards the flipped-over car. For every call that I took that had this level of danger, I hoped for the best. I always wanted to see survivors make it out of what happened to them.

I started to hear noises as I got close to the car. Though it was muffled, I swore I heard a woman's voice yelling for help.

"You hear that, right?"

My partner looked towards me, disbelief on his face even through his face covering. "Hear what?"

Our heavy breathing was louder than the yelling, but I could still hear it. "It's a woman! She's alive!"

With adrenaline running through me, I hurried even faster to the car. My partner and I worked together and with the help of some tools, we flipped the car over. I saw the outline of two people.

'We're here to help!" I yelled.

Once I was inside the car, I saw that one of the people was a baby girl in a car seat and she was unconscious but breathing. The little girl reminded me of my niece, who I was helping raise. I rushed her to the ambulance and she was sent off separately from the woman who was driving. Unfortunately, her mother passed away but I was left shocked.

"The voice I heard was a woman's," I told my partner, firm in my belief.

"It's impossible. The timing does add up. That little girl was way too young to be calling out like you said." My partner was certain that I must've heard incorrectly.

"No, I heard a woman's voice calling for help." I wasn't going to let anyone talk me out of this. I began to smile as I thought about it. I couldn't explain how I knew or how it happened, but I started to believe that something bigger was working to save that little girl. Her mother's voice spoke out to save her.

The young girl made a full recovery and went on to live with her grandparents. Her story made me cherish my relationship with my niece even more. My belief about her mother working in mysterious ways to call out for help remained true. Though she was gone at the time, she still helped save her daughter.

That call was the one that I was the most grateful to have worked late for.

MIRACLE HOUR

Ruby never could have imagined that after going to the hospital to give birth to her daughter, she would be referred to as a "miracle."

She was wheeled to the surgery room to undergo a c-section surgery. While she was nervous about it, all that Ruby cared about was that her daughter was healthy. The surgery was a success, and her baby was just as beautiful as she hoped for her to be.

Except Ruby started to experience something she did not expect. It was growing difficult for her to breathe.

"Must be a delayed reaction from the surgery," she thought to herself. That was the only explanation. She attempted to take a deep breath, but it made her cough over and over. Even her nose felt blocked.

In the recovery unit when a nurse entered her room, she asked, "May I have a tissue? I am feeling stuffy."

The nurse looked at her, almost confused.

Ruby wasn't sure what to say. But suddenly she was very tired, and that didn't seem normal. Wasn't she supposed to be feeling less groggy after the surgery? She started to drift off.

Before she could know for sure, Ruby's eyes were closed, and she was being wheeled out of the recovery room. She didn't know it at the time, but her heart had stopped beating. The doctors were working hard to revive her by any means necessary for as long as three hours.

Ruby was experiencing something extraordinary during that time. She went on to describe a situation in which she was floating along a tunnel. There were bright lights, and she made connections with spiritual beings she identified as family who passed away.

At the time, she wanted to keep going but an invisible force stopped her from doing so. This was the moment when her heart began beating again, even without any more revival efforts from the doctors.

The shock from everyone around Ruby startled her when she opened her eyes again. Her husband grasped her hand and kissed her on the cheek. "Ruby! You're alive!"

Still groggy, Ruby smiled at her husband. "How's our daughter?"

He tried to keep his questions limited. He didn't want to overwhelm his wife, but the doctors had pronounced her dead moments before her heart rate resumed on the monitor.

"She's doing great. She's resting." He smiled at Ruby.

It wasn't until later on when Ruby was holding her daughter in her arms that she shared her experience.

"I saw a lot when I was in that emergency room," she said. "It was peaceful, and I saw many relatives that passed away already. I think it was a near-death experience."

Her husband nodded. "Ruby, they pronounced you dead. Your heart stopped beating for several minutes, and your skin was gray. I was preparing my final good-bye…"

She was shocked to hear this, but their experiences matched.

"I could have passed away, I guess. But I was chosen to be here," she said.

Her daughter began to open her eyes as Ruby held her. The baby peered up at her, making Ruby's eyes fill with tears. Her daughter was the reason that she was still alive. She wasn't meant to leave her so soon. Ruby then made a promise to her newborn, stating how grateful she was to be her mother and that she would always be there for her.

LARRY'S MISSION

Larry felt like his life was slipping away from him. He'd spent years and years running from his crimes. He'd gotten into jewelry theft. It started as a small crime. While conducting remodeling work in customers' homes, Larry would steal a piece of jewelry and pawn it for extra cash to get by.

But Larry got more serious in his crimes. His name even landed on the FBI's most wanted list. At the end of his crime spree, his jewelry theft was at its worst. He did anything to keep it going, and hardly feared getting caught.

Larry was sentenced to twelve years in prison. Nobody messed with him in prison, as he was described as hulking in his size. Plus, he was covered in tattoos. At times, he was lucky that nobody messed with him. For most of his sentence, he was bitter about his life and the way it ended up. Deep down, he knew he could have done more with it. He wanted out of jail so he could go back to his theft…it was his only option. Who would hire a man who went to federal prison and was on an FBI Most Wanted list?

But everything changed for Larry one day. One of his new-found friends was moved to solitary confinement.

"I'll be here when you get out," Larry promised his friend. The plan was that he was only going to be in solitary confinement for several weeks. But not long after, Larry learned that his friend died in his jail cell.

The news changed Larry's perspective. It showed him how short life can be, and that his friend likely wouldn't have lost his life if he wasn't serving time in prison. It made Larry think of all the innocent children who find their way into a life of crime. He knew many promising friends who had gone down the path. What would his own life be like if he never started stealing?

"I need to put this into action," he thought.

Larry channeled his grief into his idea. He was on a mission to create a program for at-risk youth that would help them. He wanted to give them the support they needed to stay away from risky situations and gateways to crime.

If only he'd had such a program… or his friend… Or any of the men in the prisons across America. How much better could life be?

Larry was released and got hard at work to develop his program. He called it Lawton 911, featuring his last name. He silently worried that kids would not join his program or that parents would judge him, never letting their kids spend a minute with him.

However, Larry had the experience to teach from. He'd experienced it all and could show the kids the realities of a life full of crime. His efforts were recognized right away, and he got more support than he expected. Larry was the very first ex-convict to receive the title of "Honorary Police Officer." It was a title he never thought he wanted until he had it. The meaning of it went deep and brought a never-ending smile to his face. His mission was a success.

A DECADE OF TRAVEL

From a young age, I loved to travel. I wanted to see how the rest of the world worked. Being from Denmark, I knew there was so much to be seen outside of my home country. I dreamt of trying new foods, learning new cultural customs, and meeting people from different walks of life. At the age of 34, many of my peers were stuck in corporate jobs and unhappy. My theory about why they felt that was because they spent so much time doing the same thing every day.

I wanted to see something new each day because that would mean I would learn something new. When I started planning my travels, I knew I wanted to visit every country in the world. Had anyone done that before? After a bit of research, I learned that it had been done before. But most people utilized planes in their journey. I wanted mine to be different.

Traveling across the world was not something to be completed in a few weeks or months. Without the luxury planes, it would take a long time. But it was nothing I wanted to rush. I was ready to soak in every moment.

As I stepped foot into each new country, I vowed to spend at least twenty-four hours in each place. Most of my travel methods were by foot, car, bus, or train. Little did I know I'd sail across bodies of water on shipping containers! Thirty-seven times to be exact.

I made phone calls to my girlfriend Lu when it was possible. She even visited me a few times throughout the year. At one point, I discovered I would be stuck in West Africa for an unknown amount of time.

"What is going on?" she asked me when I gave her the news that I was stuck.

"There is an outbreak of a disease. It's called Ebola," I told her.

Lu said she heard something on the news about it. "Are you going to come back home after this? Maybe cut the trip short?" she asked.

"No, I need to keep going," I promised her. As nice

as it would be to go home, it was not the point of my traveling. Why run away when things get difficult?

The outbreak also meant she would not be able to visit me for a long time. At times, I was scared to be in other countries during events such as the Ebola outbreak. There were also times of civil unrest and difficulty with forceful governments. But I looked at these events as lessons.

My traveling lasted the span of a decade. Some countries I spent time in for months as I explored. Some hardships delayed me from moving on too, especially at strict borders. Airplanes used for travel became more and more common. At times, I struggled to find ways to travel without them. Yet I was committed to traveling in the more traditional mentions, no matter what. By the end of the journey, I was mentally exhausted but grateful for everything I experienced.

The biggest takeaway from traveling to 203 countries was that I was met with kindness in every place I went. It inspired me to be the same to those around me.

SENSE OF SECURITY

Marie Van Brittan Brown spent most of her nights working late. She was a nurse at a hospital in Queens, the same city was born. She was passionate about helping others in times of need and supporting families as they stayed with their loved ones. Most nights, she left the hospital very late or even early into the morning hours.

She remained on guard as she went home alone. Her husband, Albert, worked irregular hours as a technician who worked on various electronics. Their home was in an area with a high crime rate. Being a nurse, Marie saw firsthand what the violence of nearby neighborhoods brought into the emergency room of the hospital. It always worried her.

One night, she slipped into the dark house after work. She didn't feel much safer in her home than she did outside in the neighborhood. She decided at that moment she needed to find a way to make her home safer. There was no reason to feel like she had to hide in her own home. Marie wanted to feel at ease, whether or not her husband was home after her shifts at the hospital. To her, the first step would be finding out who was at her door if she heard knocking or other noises.

With her husband occasionally bringing home different projects, Maria saw her share of technology and tools. "I'll at least need a camera and a monitor to project the recording on," she told herself. Albert had a spare closet with items that could help her.

Marie lost track of time as she sat at the dining room table. She managed to connect the monitors with the cameras. She worked on them for weeks after work and late into the night. One night, walked past them and saw her own reflection on the screens. All she needed to do was set it up to display the camera at the door.

A few weeks later, Maria stayed up extra late. Albert came home, surprised to see his wife still up. "Why do you have all this equipment out?" he asked her.

"I'm trying to build something." She explained to Albert her idea about the cameras for the front door for security. "I've been working on this for a while now. I think what I have is promising."

Albert agreed that it was a great idea. If they became victims of a crime, there would be evidence. Part of him was shocked his wife pieced everything together so well. Albert suggested a two-way microphone and four peepholes. Together, the couple called it their surveillance system.

It took many hours of hard work and problem-solving. Some nights, Marie didn't want to stay up after a long shift at the hospital to work on it. But she promised herself at least one hour of work. Usually, once she got started, she didn't have any trouble staying focused. Marie even added a remote feature that allowed her to unlock the door from a safe distance and an emergency button to contact the police. She felt safer than ever before.

She and Albert received a patent for their invention in 1969. The surveillance device paved the way for modern security systems used in banks, office buildings, and housing complexes.

BEAR THE HERO

People were often shocked when I told them my dog saved my life. Some didn't believe that a dog could do such a thing. But Bear was special and a hero. I walked into the animal shelter with the hopes of adopting a small dog. As a lifelong dog-lover, I wanted a companion. But I wanted a dog that I thought would be easier to care for than a big dog.

I couldn't have imagined I would leave the animal shelter with a dog weighing 90 lbs and whose breed was known for working with police officers. Bear was the most beautiful German shepherd I'd ever laid eyes on, and he sure lived up to his name. Still, Bear was a gentle giant with nothing but love and loyalty in his heart.

He proved this to me when I was gardening outside one summer afternoon. I was hitting my limit with the heat but was too stubborn to go inside. Bear was nudging his nose into my leg as if to alert me to go inside and cool down.

"Not yet. Just a few more minutes, Bear," I told him and patted his head. He continued to nuzzle me.

Then my vision started to fade, and I rolled onto the ground from where I crouched. Bear ran over, and all I could remember was his black face and brown eyes. He was watching over me with concern. I had a history of seizures and knew by the shaking of my body that I was experiencing one. Bear had never seen me in such a helpless state.

I was knocked out for a little while but then had enough strength to look around the yard for Bear. But he was nowhere to be found. Did I scare him off? Did he somehow run out of the gate of the backyard? What if nobody came back for me? I feared I may be too weak to get inside on my own.

I couldn't be sure how much time passed but it felt like a long time. When I fully regained consciousness, I wondered if I was dreaming. Bear was pulling a man in uniform into the backyard by his pants.

"Ma'am are you okay?!" he yelled.

"I need some help!" I called back. Bear ran to my side, sitting between the man and me. I was so relieved to see Bear and the stranger.

The man was an animal control officer who spotted Bear running from door to door, then darted to him. He called 9-11 and an ambulance arrived. Bear rode with me to the hospital and I realized he must've sensed my seizure coming on and he ran out of the yard to find help. Bear was never trained in how to detect seizures but somehow knew. Even after the fall, Bear would nuzzle me in the same way he did in the garden that day. That showed me I needed to prepare for a potential seizure. Bear would stay by my side for as long as I needed him.

Later on, Bear was presented the 30th National Hero Dog Award by the Society of Prevention for Cruelty to Animals. My shelter dog was recognized as a hero for saving my life, exactly how he deserved to be. Bear was the biggest blessing in my life.

WAITING FOR A LIFETIME

For as long as I could remember, I wanted a daughter. So when I gave birth to my daughter Carlina in July of 1987, I vowed it was the best day of my life. We lived in New York and the first few weeks weren't easy, though Carlina was everything I wanted her to be. When she was almost three weeks old, Calina fell ill.

She had an infection and fever. I was so worried about my newborn daughter and rushed her to the hospital. I feared the worst when the doctor told me they wanted to admit her.

"Don't worry, she is in great hands," one of the nurses promised me.

As concerned as I was about my daughter, I let those words sink into my mind. Carlina was exactly where she needed to be. She was receiving the medical care she needed for her infection and we'd be back home in no time.

But the next day I was shocked to learn she was not in the NICU anymore. I demanded the hospital look into the surveillance and filed a police report. I cried, but also told myself it couldn't be true. My daughter would be found soon. Someone provided a tip about seeing a strange woman around the NICU for several hours. Most thought she was another parent, but the hospital had reasons to believe that she took Carlina.

"I don't know what to do," I told the doctors when I had a meeting with them.

"The best thing you can do is wait for more information or someone to see Carlina and report it." Their advice seemed impossible to follow.

I did what they said and I waited days, weeks, and months. There was no news about the mystery woman or Carlina. Years began to pass, and I grieved for my daughter. But I still had a flicker of hope that I would see her again one day. I truly believed I would see her and hug her. I just couldn't know when. I liked to look at is a surprise.

A friend asked me how I had such strong faith in it happening.

"I just know. A mother knows. I will see my daughter again one day," I explained to her. It was a feeling I couldn't describe in words. There was no doubt in my mind. I could only hope it was sooner than later that I saw her again.

It took 23 years for my belief to come true. But I never gave up hope. A woman named Ann got in contact with me after seeing photos of an infant reported missing. She was convinced the photos were of her, and she never felt like she resembled her family. She said she could be the baby from the report.

From the moment we spoke, I knew it was Carlina. We were reunited and she had the same beautiful dark eyes as she did when she was born. "Ann" was Carlina, I knew it in my bones. My faith brought me through the pain and questioning. Seeing my daughter once again was the miracle I prayed for all of those years. The surprise came true. Carlina was proud to call me her mother.

THE SELF-SERVICE STORE

Clarence Saunders loved to think about how he could redesign things in his daily life. He was a grocer who always worked traditionally with his store. His customers would visit with their grocery list in hand, and Clarence would fill a few bags for them. The process worked well but Clarence believed that there was a way to make the process of grocery shopping more automated.

His dream store would change the way customers shopped. Instead of them handing him a list to grab the items, Clarence had a better idea.

"Customers will walk through the store and make their own selections of items," he explained to his family.

"The products will be set out in the store and organized, but ultimately they will do their own shopping."

His family and friends couldn't imagine a store that operated in such a way. Especially when Clarence told them another idea he had. "One day, I'd like to see the store have different departments. We'd have our own butcher and bakery."

That idea seemed even more shocking with how many specialty retail shops there were in down. Clarence began drafting the designs of his new store layout. In 1916, he began a full remodel. The new design game him plenty of space to set out the products to be displayed for customers to choose their items.

One of his friends came to the store when the renovations were opening. "Nobody is going to want to do this themselves! How are they going to carry their items around before paying?!" he asked.

Clarence already had that figured out. Next to his automatic cash register, Clarence had a stack of baskets.

"They can take a basket when they arrive and carry it with their items. It is simple."

His friend didn't look fully convinced yet.

"I already have some regular customers who are interested in it. I think it will take time to learn, but customers are excited." Clarence loved his friend, but he was ready to prove him wrong.

On September 11, 1916, the self-service grocery store officially opened. Clarence called it Piggly Wiggly. He'd designed the layout of the store to be as functional as possible. It had a lobby in the front, a main pathway to the sales area, and a rear stockroom.

In a short amount of time, Clarence could see the success of his store and the new process. Piggly Wiggly began stocking four times the variety of products that the average grocery store held. For the first time, customers had options to choose from and could see the products right in front of them before making a decision to purchase. To Clarence, it was a win-win. Less work for him and more control for the customers.

Clarence successfully received a patent for the design of his store and only five years later, 615 Piggly Wiggly stores were open across 40 states in the US. Clarence didn't let the fear of a new design or operating method hold him back. His idea for convenience permanently changed the way grocery stores operated for the coming years.

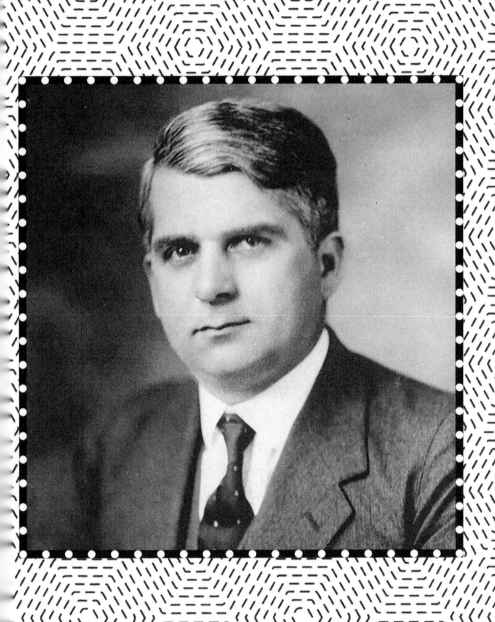

REVENGE FRIES

"The customer said the French fries were too thick and mushy," one of the serves said and passed me the plate.

I was instantly frustrated at the comment. "Seriously?" I picked up the french fries and ate one. I always received compliments on the French fries I cooked. They were the most popular side dish on our menu. The ones on the customer's plate were no different.

"What should I tell him? He refused to eat any more of them." The server seemed intimidated by the difficult customer.

I gave him a wicked grin. The day was not going smoothly for me, as I woke up late and the restaurant was understaffed. "I'll make him a very special batch of his own French fries!"

The server backed away, uneasy with my idea of revenge.

I sliced the potatoes as thinly as possible and dumped them into the fryer. I let them cook twice as long as I did the French fries. "If he wants them crispy, he will get them crispy!"

Maybe I was overreacting a little bit, but I was offended that someone had a complaint about the delicious French fries I was known for cooking. I pulled the thin fries out of the fryer, noticing a few tips of them were burnt on the edges. I added extra salt and then passed the plate to the server when he returned.

"Crispy fries, just as requested!" I called out. I couldn't wait to hear the customer's response. The thin, salty, crunchy fries that he asked for would prove how much better my traditional ones were. He would regret calling them mushy and too thick.

I paced the kitchen for a few minutes, tending to my grill and fryer and even cleaning up a bit. There was no sign of the server returning with a replacement side dish. When the server did return to the kitchen, I stopped him.

"I take it he is too scared to complain about the new fries? He must hate them even more. I'm surprised he's not begging for the old ones yet!" I said to the server, laughing.

"He actually really likes them. He wants to thank you for making such a perfect dish."

My jaw fell open. That customer must be playing a joke on me. The server lead me to the table, and the man had a satisfied smile on his face.

"I've never had fries like that before. They were delicious and so crispy!"

"Oh…thank you," I said as I looked around the room. "I didn't think you could even taste the potatoes anymore."

The customer shook his head. "The flavor is still there, but no mushiness. Perfection! I'm going to tell all my friends about these. Don't be surprised if you get similar requests."

I couldn't believe it, but in the following weeks, customers flooded in asking for extra crispy fries. I decided they needed their own menu name. I called them Saratoga Chips, based on my hometown of Saratoga Springs.

They were a hit, and local restaurants began making similar chips. I even got a call from my mother that there were thin, fried potatoes in a cookbook she had.

The side dish that was made to seek revenge, turned out to become a favorite of customers across the city and state. Eventually, chips became a packaged snack enjoyed by all.

THE SOLO ROW

Three thousand miles was a long way to row on her own. But Mariam's passion was rowing. She loved to be alone on the water, while taking in the views each day and keeping herself company. To her, rowing across the Atlantic Ocean would be a dream come true.

She also wanted to raise money during her rowing for an organization she was passionate about called Wellbeing of Women and Mind out of East Yorkshire. She knew with the help of sponsors she could raise more money by rowing than making her own single donation.

She set out on the water, saying goodbye to her friends and family. They admitted they would miss her on the holidays because she would be rowing through Christmas and New Year's, but it didn't bother Mariam.

Christmas 2022 would be like no other she'd had. "It'll be a holiday I never forget! The one I spent on the Atlantic Ocean," she told them.

In her boat, she brought her own food, water, and safety equipment. About one week into her rowing, sleep deprivation struck Mariam first. Most nights she was only sleeping a couple of hours. Her energy was being used up even quicker as she was rowing against very harsh winds most days. The warm temperatures were no help either. The average day was 86 degrees during the day.

"I'm going to lose the record," she said to herself over the crashing of waves onto the boat. The winds were so harsh that she rowed for eighteen hours straight and traveled less than the miles by the end. She fought off the tears, let herself rest, and continued trying. Mariam had to accept that she needed to keep rowing, whether or not she would make the record of the fastest time.

Hunger and dehydration took a toll on her body, too. She could only eat a small amount of the food she packed with her. She couldn't waste any of it, knowing that she would need it even more by the end of the trip.

It wasn't all difficult, though. Mariam's favorite parts of the day were sunrise and sunset. Each one was unique in its own pattern and colors, and the view she had from far away from land was priceless. Mariam also spotted marine life she'd never seen before. She saw sharks, dolphins, and numerous species of birds and fish. She lost track of all the amazing life living beneath her and her boat.

The last ten miles were the most difficult of the trip. Her exhaustion, hunger and dehydration were at their peak. Mariam felt like her body and mind were hanging on by a thread. But she pressed on, knowing she was so close and her goal was still within her reach. In the last mile, a surge of energy took over her and she even began calling out for her friends and family waiting for her at the finish line.

Mariam struck land and was awarded with her new record: the fastest female to row across the Atlantic. It took 59 days and 3,000 miles to reach land again. But Mariam made history at only twenty-three years old and made a substantial donation to her charity of choice.

ASTRONOMICAL SUCCESS

From a very young age, Sara Seager was fascinated by Physics. It became her favorite subject in school, and her favorite activity was to look at the moon through their telescope. They spent many nights together looking at the night sky. While in high school, she learned that being an astrophysicist could actually be a career.

"Dad, I know what I want to go to college for. I want to study astronomy," she told him.

But her father didn't express much support for the idea. "I don't think that's a good career path," he told her. "You need to become a doctor or a lawyer. Those are more stable careers."

Sara was disappointed that she didn't have his support but also wondered if maybe he was right about the stability. Still, by the time Sara entered the University of Toronto, she was excited to pursue a degree in something she liked to call her "first love," which was astronomy. It was the same subject she later pursued a Ph.D. in at Harvard.

The doubt from her father gave her the drive to create even more accomplishments for herself. She wanted to prove to the world that she could have a promising career after studying astronomy. She also wanted to prove that her findings were meaningful to the field and the future of space study. She had a lot to prove for a woman working in the field. Prior to Sara entering it, it was established mostly by men. In many ways, Sara had the odds stacked against her.

The doubts didn't stop there. While in her doctorate program, her supervisor encouraged her to study exoplanets, very similar to the planet Jupiter. At the time, many scientists had different beliefs about what created the planets. Some even told Sara that the claims she made as a result of her studies would never hold up after more research.

Despite all of the doubt, she continued her studies on the exoplanets and grew her theories about them.

She worked with a supportive team after her Ph.D. program that also studied exoplanets. Together, the group co-discovered the first light detection from an exoplanet. Eventually, Sara began working with the Kepler Space Telescope and discovered 715 planets. Much of her research contributed largely to the modern understanding of space. All of those who doubted her original ideas about exoplanets learned that she was right all along. The research that supported her thesis during her studies served to be important. Her family also realized how prominent space study became over the years, in many ways because of Sara's research accomplishments.

Sara often thought of herself as a little girl who loved to look through the telescope. She became a professional woman who got to do the exact same thing as her career. Even through the doubt of her father and her fellow students and colleagues, she became known as an important woman in astronomy who left a lasting mark on the field. She also worked as a professor and helped shape the future of students who had a deep love for space.

GETTING BACK IN THE WATER

"Will I ever surf again?" Bethany was lying in a hospital bed after an accident in the ocean. The thought of giving up her passion broke her heart. It still felt unreal.

"Never say never," her mother said and comforted her daughter. She couldn't give her an official answer yet.

All Bethany knew was surfing. She began paddling on a surfboard at the age of 5. By 8, she was enrolling in surfing competitions. Other competitors, judges, and professionals in the sport saw a promising future for her. There was even one judge who pulled Bethany's parents aside after a heated competition win. "If she keeps up with surfing, she could become a professional," the judge told them.

Becoming a professional surfer sounded like a dream to Bethany. At thirteen years old, she thought that would be the most exciting career path. But the injury was going to change everything because the accident caused Bethany to lose her arm.

She always knew the risks of paddling into the ocean. But she never would have guessed she would become a victim of a shark attack. Her recovery was slow to start. Bethany underwent multiple surgeries to repair where her arm once was, and she lost nearly 60% of her blood. Her recovery extended past the hotel room too, as she had to learn how to do everything. One arm meant her clothes would fit differently. She would have to accept that she would always look different. Her friends may treat her differently and she would have to give up some things. Still, all Bethany could think about surfing.

"When can I try to surf?" she asked her parents regularly. "I want to get back in the water."

Bethany's parents were proud to hear their daughter confidently speak. Her vow to return to surfing was inspirational to everyone around her. Once her doctor cleared her to go into the ocean, Bethany was ready. She had a relationship with the ocean and trusted that she could return to her favorite sport.

She practiced paddling through the water day after day. All she had was her right arm to propel her through the water. With half the strength she normally had, she still made it over the waves. Bethany's family watched her from the shoreline. They were nervous as expected, but she adjusted better than they imagined. Bethany found herself catching waves and she felt as good as she did before the accident. She still tumbled into the water occasionally or had a large wave crash on her, but that was normal for surfing!

Bethany resumed competing. The community rallied around her, showing their support for the young girl. Losing her arm did not hold her back, and Bethany competed in all of the competitions she qualified for. Some were local, some were much larger that she had to travel to. Her fellow surfers treated her just the same and Bethany still felt the competitive drive she loved out on the water. Bethany even competed and won a national title only two years after the accident. Losing a limb did not slow down Bethany's love for surfing. Instead, it showed how strong and dedicated she was to her sport. When most would let go of their dream, Bethany only held on tighter.

SCAN

FOR YOUR FREE
DOWNLOAD

Printed in Great Britain
by Amazon

28706496R00064